SELENE GOES HOME

SELENE
GOES HOME
by Lucy Diggs

illustrated by
Emily Arnold McCully

Atheneum   1989   New York

Atheneum
Macmillan Publishing Company
866 Third Avenue, New York, NY 10022
Collier Macmillan Canada, Inc.
First Edition   Printed in the United States of America

10   9   8   7   6   5   4   3   2   1

Library of Congress Cataloging-in-Publication Data
Diggs, Lucy.
Selene goes home / by Lucy Diggs; illustrated by Emily Arnold
McCully. — 1st ed.   p.   cm.
Summary: Selene the cat does not like her mistress's new home aboard
a houseboat and returns to her old home with the help of a
pesky sea gull.   ISBN 0-689-31464-7
[1. Cats—Fiction. 2. Moving, Household—Fiction. 3. Houseboats—
Fiction.] I. McCully, Emily Arnold, ill. II. Title.
PZ7.D5765Se 1989   Fic—dc19   88-7363 CIP AC

For Lyn Gustafson,
who has read many stories to many children.
With love and appreciation.

SELENE GOES HOME

Chapter One

For Selene, the twenty-first of September started out as a usual day. She ate her breakfast, as usual; then she went up the hill behind the house to hunt, as usual. The sun beamed warm rays on her back. The sky spread a wide canopy of blue over her. She was thinking about catching a mouse, or perhaps a bird. Or a snake with bright green stripes, slithering through the grass.

When she caught something, she

1

took it in her teeth and trotted down to the house with it. A nice present for Margaret, her owner. In the house, she deposited it in a place where Margaret would be sure to find it—at the foot of Margaret's bed, or beside the fireplace in the living room. For some reason, Margaret didn't seem to like the presents. But Selene kept bringing them anyway. Perhaps Margaret would like the next one.

Selene liked to hunt on the hill behind the house. She also liked to race through the tall grass and pounce on leafy shadows; to scamper up and down trees and stalk thistles skittering in the wind. When she was tired, she'd curl up and listen to the trees telling her stories of the olden times, in their rustly, whispery voices.

This particular morning Selene romped up the hill to a spot near the pear tree. There, she crouched low and crept forward through the tall grass, looking and listening, waiting to catch sight of a lizard scuttling across her path, or to hear the sound of a mouse or a mole. She moved ever so slowly, and very patiently; waiting, looking, listening.

"*Rrrrumble! Eeurk. Screeech!*"

The unusual noise from down by the house made Selene jump into the air with alarm. Then she ran to investigate it.

In the driveway she saw a big white truck. Four men in white coveralls climbed out of the truck and went into the house. Who could they be? What were they doing? Selene scampered down the hill to find out more.

In the kitchen, one man was wrapping plates in paper and putting them into a cardboard box. All over the house, wherever Selene went, it seemed a man in white coveralls was packing something into a box and sealing it with tape.

Selene ran to Margaret's room and dived into the closet. There, in the farthest, dimmest back corner, she hid between a pair of sneakers. What if they packed *her* into a box?

In the closet it was dark and quiet, though she could hear the voices and footsteps of the men in the rest of the

house. She trembled and curled herself into a very small ball. Then she began to think: She didn't know exactly what was happening, but the thing to do when faced with a dangerous situation was not to hide from it, but to be brave. If someone came for her, she would attack.

The next thing she knew, the closet door opened wide. A huge pair of hands reached inside and took an armful of Margaret's shirts off the closet pole. The hands reached inside again and took another armful. Soon all the clothes were gone. The hands swept several pairs of shoes from the floor of the closet. The sneakers where Selene was lying in wait would be next. She crouched low and pounced, landing quite near a big foot.

"Oh, look!" the man in the white coveralls said over his shoulder. "A cat! Isn't she pretty?" He bent down to stroke her, but Selene did not want to be admired. She wanted to be respected. She bristled her fur and bared her teeth, but the man only smiled. She ran out of the room and down the hall to find Margaret.

"Be careful with that," Margaret said to one of the men. "That music box belonged to my grandmother."

Selene rubbed her side against Margaret's leg. Margaret stepped backward and nearly squashed her tail. Selene yowled and ran outside. What had happened to Margaret? She'd never stepped on Selene before. Even when she was busy, she'd take time to rub Selene's ears or stroke her back.

Selene sat up on the hill and watched the house. For hours and hours the men went back and forth, carrying boxes and furniture out of the house and packing them into a truck. Selene was worried.

Nothing like this had ever happened before. What was going to happen next?

In the afternoon the men closed up the back of the truck and drove away. When the truck disappeared down the driveway, Selene decided it was safe to go back inside the house. But nothing inside the house was the way it was supposed to be. In the living room, only the rug remained. In the dining room, only the big

sideboard. In the bedroom, nothing ex-
cept a large spiderweb in the corner of the
closet. Selene was too upset to enjoy this
discovery. She went to the kitchen. Nothing in the kitchen. Even her bowl was
gone. Now what would she do for dinner?
Meowing mournfully, Selene went into
the living room to curl up in her bed in
the window seat. All the soft, cozy pillows
were gone. She jumped into the window
seat and settled uncomfortably on the hard
boards.

"Selene!" Margaret called. "Here, kitty,
kitty!"

Selene almost jumped down to cud-
dle in Margaret's arms, but then she decided it would be more prudent to wait
and see what was on Margaret's mind. Her
voice had a shrill note to it, and that usu-
ally meant she was going to do something
that Selene didn't enjoy—like sprinkle her

with flea powder or trim her claws or give her a bath.

Oh no! Margaret was holding the cat carrier. Selene hissed at it. That carrier

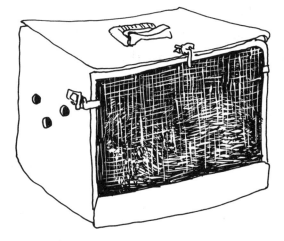

meant trouble. Margaret would stuff her inside and take her to the vet. In the vet's waiting room, it stank of dog and stranger-cats, of medicine and antiseptic. In the examining room it was even worse. The vet poked her with his hands and jabbed her with needles.

Hissing at the carrier turned out to be a mistake, because it made Margaret look in her direction.

"There you are, Selene. Come, kitty, kitty, kitty!"

Selene jumped down and ran for it, but Margaret caught her and stuck her in the carrier. She took her out to the car and put her in the backseat.

Selene yowled in misery. She yowled while Margaret backed the car around and drove down the driveway. She yowled when the car turned onto the street. She yowled while the car rolled along the road. At last the car came to a stop and she yowled even louder, thinking about the dogs and the horrible smells at the vet's.

Margaret lifted the carrier out of the car and Selene forgot to yowl. What a strange smell! It wasn't the vet's. What was it?

Chapter Two

The carrier bounced and lurched in Margaret's hands as she walked along. Selene crouched on the bottom, sniffing furiously.

At last, Margaret set the carrier down and opened its door. Selene bolted out and ran. Up some stairs, into a little room at the top of the stairs, up onto a ledge. The ledge was in front of a window and she looked out, trying to figure out where she was. What she saw made her jump

13

straight up in the air with surprise. Tall,
thin poles jutted up into the sky. Ropes
slapped against the poles. They rocked
back and forth, bobbed up and down.
The shelf where Selene sat swayed and
rocked. Across the way, large house-look-
ing things swayed and bobbed. She
looked down and saw, instead of grass or
dirt, a blue, rippling surface that bounced
the sun's rays back into her eyes.

A large white bird with a yellow beak

and gray-tipped wings settled on the roof not two feet away from Selene. He lifted his yellow, webbed feet, strutting back and forth on the roof right in front of her. Then he marched up to the window and glared at her. Selene glared back. He was not intimidated, and Selene, all of a sudden, felt less like a brave hunter and more like someone who wanted things to be usual and comfortable.

"Margaret!" she called. "Take me home! Please?"

Margaret came and stroked her back. "How do you like your new home, Selene? What do you think of living on a houseboat?"

Selene told her that this was not her home, but Margaret did not understand. She carried Selene downstairs, out onto the deck, telling her she would soon get used to it. "You'll like it," she said. "Smell

the clean salt air? See the sailboat out in the channel? And look at that sea gull! See how gracefully he soars?" Margaret pointed to the same big white bird Selene had just seen. Now he circled overhead, filling the air with squawks and screeches. Selene shuddered and went back upstairs. Perhaps it was a bad dream. Perhaps she would wake up in her own bed in the window seat at home. The roses would be tapping at the window and the oak trees would be casting long dawn shadows on the grass.

But next morning, when Selene woke up, she discovered that she was still in this strange new place that Margaret called the houseboat. Wherever she looked, she saw water and boats and birds. She heard sea gulls screeching, ducks quacking, and waves slapping.

Day after day, Selene sat on the deck of the houseboat and dreamed about the house on the hill where she was born. She

dreamed of the roses tapping at her windowpane, squirrels scampering up trees, and dragonflies droning in the soft air. She thought so hard about where she would like to be—and was not—that she scarcely noticed where she was: She didn't see the mallard duck family that swam by almost every day, or the white sails billowing in the wind, or the tantalizing tangles of ropes that dropped between the houseboat and the dock. She only kept on dreaming. . . .

Bonk!

A hard object whacked Selene on the head. She jumped to her feet and looked up. The big white sea gull cackled at her from his perch on top of the piling. It wasn't the first time he had done such a thing. Sometimes he swooped from high in the sky, plummeting down like an arrow, with his yellow beak aimed right at

her. Then, at the last minute, he leveled off and flew away. Other times he sat on the piling and stared at her with his bright, beady eyes until her skin prickled. And often he circled overhead so even her dreams about earth and trees had sea gull noises in them.

This time the gull swooped down and took another mussel from the side of the houseboat. He cracked it on the piling and dropped the shell down, in her direction. Selene jumped out of the way, and it

landed on the deck next to the one that had just hit her on the head.

"Quit it!" she yelled.

"Mussels are my favorite food," the gull squawked.

"You needn't drop the shells on my deck."

"I will if I want," said the gull. "You can't stop me." With that, he took off from the piling and flew away.

What a rude bird, Selene thought, annoyed by his sass and the way he taunted her.

The next thing she knew, he was cruising by right in front of her, smirking with self-importance.

Selene had had enough. She gathered her hind legs beneath her and sprang with a mighty spring. She hurtled through the air and landed directly on the gull's back. She dug her claws into his back and

reached for his neck with her teeth. He scuttled in the water, screamed and squawked and beat his wings furiously. Selene did not let go. He thrashed and turned and yelled at her, but still she did not let go. He scrabbled at the salt sea with his wings and his webbed feet. She dug her claws deeper into his back.

Finally, he turned upside down in the water. Selene could not breathe. She lost her grip on the gull's back and plummeted down, down through the dark, cold water. Then, churning her paws, she struggled to the surface. She spluttered and gasped,

breathing the air with great relief. The waves bounced her up and down. Paddling hard, she swam to the side of the house-boat. After climbing aboard, she shook and shook herself, trying to get the water out of her coat. Presently, she sat down

23

and began to remove the salt and seaweed from her coat with her tongue.

While she was working on her coat, a splashing sound in the water made her look up. That gull again! If she hadn't felt so bedraggled, she would have jumped at him again.

You! she started to yell. Just get out of here! Leave me alone! But he swam closer and stopped a few feet in front of her. He cocked his head to the left in a quizzical way. She cocked hers to the right.

"I didn't think you would do that," he said in a voice with less screech than usual. "No cat has ever done that before."

"Well," she sniffed, feeling rather proud of herself, "I'm not an ordinary cat."

"Why did you do it?" he asked.

"Why did you?" she asked back, although she wanted to say: You started it! You pestered and provoked me! You taunted and teased me. You asked for it, buddy. . . . She decided not to say any of those things because they sounded— well—provocative, and it was rather nice to be having a conversation instead of a fight.

"Oh well. . . ." He shrugged a wing. "For fun, you might say."

"And what about me? Did you ever

think about how I felt? *Fun!??"*

"Sure. I like to dive and swoop. Catch things. Sometimes for fun, sometimes because I'm hungry. Don't suppose you've ever done anything like that?"

"Certainly not." She was about to start explaining to him what a calm and peaceful nature she had, how what she mostly wanted to do was nap and dream—which she would do if he were not constantly disturbing her. She was about to tell him that he was mean and selfish, that he ought to consider the feelings of others, at least once in a while—when she remembered about the things she used to catch when she lived on the land. How she did it mostly for fun. And how Margaret didn't seem to like it much—how *they* probably didn't like it much.

However, she didn't see why he had to know about such things in her past.

27

"Anyway," she said, "everyone has their limits. How can I be expected to sit here day after day with nothing to do and no one to talk to?"

"You don't like it here?" asked the gull. "Why, this is the most wonderful place in the world! Nothing to do? You can go clamming and musseling. You can go swimming and diving, hitch a ride on the mast of a boat, or the bow. It's glorious to ride along with the waves parting before you and the cool spray in your face. . . ."

"Those are sea gull sorts of things," Selene snapped, feeling rather grumpy. "It's all very well for you to say it's wonderful. You *want* to be here. It's where you belong."

The gull paddled backward, cocking his head again thoughtfully. "Where do *you* want to be?"

"Home," Selene replied with no hesi-

tation at all, longing to run through the tall grass, to leap and play with the dancing shadows, to smell the earth and hear the whispering of the trees. She told the gull all about the way it was at the house on the hill, and when she was finished he looked even more thoughtful.

"Sounds nice," he said. "Why don't you go there?"

"Because I don't know where it is. And I don't know how to get there."

"I bet I could find it," he said. "From the air it's easy to find things."

"So what?" Selene said. "I can't fly."

"But I can," said the gull, looking pleased with himself and lifting his wings partway away from his sides as if he were about to demonstrate.

"So what?" she snapped, feeling even grumpier. All birds could fly. It was silly of him to be so proud of something that came with who he was.

Then he surprised her again. Surprised her so much she almost fell off the
deck. He swam very close and said in a
low, confidential tone, "So? So I can take
you."

Selene wanted to jump up in the air,
turn a somersault, cavort with joy at the
idea of actually going home. At the same
time, she was so embarrassed that she'd
been thinking such unkind thoughts that
her reply came out in a bumbling, disor-
derly way. Among the stammers and stut-
ters, however, she did manage to tell him
that she would appreciate it, she'd be very

grateful, and thank you, and would he really?

"I will," he assured her, "if you promise me one thing." Selene was about to promise anything when she noticed that his eyes were glittering with a hint of his old look. She was afraid that he was teasing her again.

"What is it?" she asked, hoping fervently that it was something she would be able to do.

"Promise not to stick your claws in my back. They hurt."

That was easy. "I promise," she answered with relief.

"Sure you want to go, though? It won't be much fun around here without you to dive at and drop shells on and . . ."

"Why, you . . . you!"

"Just teasing," he laughed. Then he swam close to the deck, so it would be easy for Selene to get on his back. She leaped as lightly and softly as she knew how. The gull turned his head and said, "Thank you. Off we go, now!"

He churned his feet in the water, swimming faster and faster, picking up speed until they were skimming the surface of the waves. Then he beat his wings up and down with strong, powerful strokes and they were airborne. The wind whistled in Selene's ears and riffled her fur. She crouched low on the gull's back and held

on tightly, making sure not to stick him with her claws. As they climbed higher Selene's heart soared, too: She was going home! Soon the bay was behind them and they flew over city streets, where the houses looked like toys; they flew over the tops of trees and through wispy tendrils of clouds, on and on into the rosy evening sky.

Chapter Three

"There it is! There it is!" Selene exclaimed. "Just fly right . . . down . . . *there*!!! There's my house!"

The gull landed at the foot of the driveway and Selene jumped off his back. She breathed in the sweet smells of the earth, quivering with pleasure. It was good to feel the earth beneath her pads and to see the trees and flowers. She bounded up the driveway toward the house, singing a little song to herself:

Oh, I'm happy to be here
I'm full of great good cheer
To see the trees and hear the bees
To smell sweet peas and feel the breeze.

Did you ever think that a cat could fly
Over the bay and through the sky
To the house on the hill
    where she longed to be
Far away from the deep salt sea?

Home at last. . . .

She continued on up the drive, but her happy coming-home song stopped singing in her head. She came to a halt, wondering what was wrong. Then she remembered that without the sea gull she wouldn't be there. She'd been so overcome with happiness that she'd forgotten all about him. When she turned around, he was still standing at the bottom of the drive, looking oddly out of place.

"Hey," she called, "Thank you, thank

you very much!"

"My pleasure," he called back. "Good luck! And good-bye."

For some reason, Selene didn't want to tell him good-bye. Instead she decided to sing some more of her song. She started up the hill again, but this time, instead of her song, she heard the buzzing of the bees and the rustling of the trees. She raced the rest of the way up the hill toward the house. There she stopped on the front lawn, trying to decide what to do first. Visit the window seat in the living room? Or perhaps the swing on the front porch? The front-porch swing was another of her favorite spots. Or maybe she'd go straight up the hill to see . . .

A huge dog with a long gray coat and fierce brown eyes tore around the corner of the house, barking ferociously. Selene raced for the nearest tree and scrambled up the trunk faster than she'd ever climbed anything in her life. When she was high enough to be safe, she bristled her fur until she was twice her normal size, bared her teeth, and hissed.

"Scram!" he barked. "No stray cats allowed here."

"I'm not a stray cat. This is my house. I was born here."

"I don't care where you were born. This is *my* house now. You come out of that tree and I'll have you for dinner."

"You come any closer and I'll claw your eyes out," Selene retaliated. She sounded braver than she felt. The dog was huge and frightening. He jumped and clawed at the trunk of the tree, barking impatiently. And that gave Selene an idea. The dog was a lot bigger than she was, but she was almost certain that she was more patient. She settled into a crook of

the tree and waited for him to go away. While she was waiting she looked around. She noticed ugly green curtains covering the window by her window seat and that someone had forgotten to water the rose-bush. Its leaves drooped and the ground beneath it was littered with petals. She noticed a strange car parked in the driveway and an orange tabby cat curled up on the front-porch swing.

The sun slipped away behind the mountain, fog blew up the valley, and the lawn fell into deep shadow. The dog tired of waiting and went into the house. Selene noted this with satisfaction. Of course she was more patient than he was. The orange tabby jumped off the swing and went inside, too. Lights came on. Smells of dinner cooking wafted through the air. Inside the house she could see one person sitting in the living room, reading the evening paper. Another stood in the kitchen, stirring a pot. They looked nothing like Margaret. Selene was tired and hungry and thirsty and cold. She was lonely and forlorn and bewildered and miserable. If she tried to go in, those people would probably say, "Scram!" just as their mean dog had.

Selene thought about the cheery fire that would be crackling in the wood-burning stove at the houseboat, and the dinner Margaret would have set out in her dish. She thought of the gentle rocking of the houseboat, and how nice it would be to

curl up in Margaret's lap and listen to the *su-lap, su-lap* of the waves outside. More than anything, that's where she wanted to be. In the morning, she resolved, I'll go. With this somewhat consoling thought, she made herself as comfortable as she could and went to sleep. Behind her, lights winked out in the house—the house that used to be her home, but was no longer.

When morning came Selene was still tired and hungry and thirsty and cold. She was also stiff and sore. Looking down, she saw that the dog and cat were nowhere to be seen. She climbed out of the tree and ran down the drive to the road.

She looked up the road to the right and wondered if that way would take her to the houseboat. She looked to the left and wondered if *that* was the way. She sat down and pondered. She didn't know which way to go.

She looked to the right again and noticed that the road climbed up. She didn't want to go up the mountain; she wanted to go down, to the sea. She turned left and trotted down the road. It was a pleasant road that wound along beside a creek. Something told Selene she was going in the right direction. Then the road came into a town. Streets branched off in every direction. Now which way should she go?

She stopped and addressed a large tortoiseshell cat who sunned himself on the front steps of a house.

"Is this the way to the sea?" Selene asked.

"I don't know," replied the tortoiseshell cat. "I've never been there." He stretched and yawned and settled back on the step. "Nor would I want to, I'm sure."

Selene walked on. She asked directions of a raven on a telephone pole, a

man at a gas station, a white terrier on a leash. The raven and the terrier said they didn't know the way, and the gas station attendant didn't understand her.

She sat down beside a juniper bush, feeling quite discouraged.

"What's wrong?" someone asked in a high, hesitant voice.

Selene looked all around, trying to locate the voice. Then she noticed a shadow, or a *something*, underneath the juniper bush.

45

A skinny calico cat with matted fur crawled out from under the bush. "Can I help? What's wrong?" she asked again in the same wispy voice.

"Nothing." Selene started to walk off, but where was she to go? This calico cat was the first being she'd met all day who had taken an interest in her. "I'm lost," Selene confessed. "Do you know the way to the sea?"

"What's the sea?" asked the calico cat.

Selene had been hoping for help and comfort. And here she was, confronted with this know-nothing ignoramus. "Don't you know anything?" she snapped. "It's where I live."

"You have a place to live? Aren't you lucky!"

"Everyone has a place to live," Selene sniffed. "If only they could find it," she muttered to herself.

"I don't."

"Nonsense," said Selene.

"No, it's true," said the calico cat.

"No family? No place to live?" Selene didn't believe it.

"Once I did," replied the calico cat, "and it was a wonderful family. Then one day they all got into the car and drove away. Of course, I thought they would come back—they often went away for a day or two. So I waited. I waited for days and days, and sometimes I was positive they'd returned. I heard them calling, 'Esther? Where are you? How are you?' They called me Esther because of these apricot parts in my coat. You see how they look like shooting stars? Esther means star in Hebrew."

Selene nodded politely, but it was hard to see anything as pretty as a star in Esther's coat, it was so matted and bedraggled. "But you just imagined they'd come back? Or dreamed it?"

Esther nodded. "Because they never did. After a while I stopped waiting and went to look for them. I looked and looked, but I couldn't find them. I'm still looking, but I get tired and . . ."

"And you say they were wonderful? I think only a terrible family would do a thing like that." Selene was indignant.

"Maybe they couldn't take me," Esther said. "Maybe there was a reason. Maybe . . ."

"There can't be a good-enough reason." Selene was so incensed she was almost yelling. "When *my* owner moved, she took me with her."

"Then what are you doing here? Why are you lost?"

"Oh, well. Never mind." Selene was ashamed. She was beginning to think how fortunate she was, and how perhaps she had not appreciated Margaret or the houseboat. In order to avoid the issue, she asked Esther, "How long have you been living by yourself?"

"I don't know," Esther answered. "Quite a long time, I think. I sleep under bushes and eat scraps out of garbage cans. It's not so bad."

"Sounds pretty bad to me," Selene said. "Wouldn't you like a warm, dry place to sleep? The same place every day? And food in your dish? A lap to curl up in?"

"Yes, I would." Esther said, sounding wistful.

"Would you like to come with me?" Selene asked. "I have a home that's big enough for two of us."

"I would. But what about your owner? Some people don't like cats. They throw things at you and yell 'Get out of here!' She might not like me."

"Yes, she will. She likes cats. She likes *me*. Come on, let's go." Selene was on her feet, ready to head down the road.

Esther hung back. "You said you didn't know the way."

"I'll find the way." Selene was filled with determination. She'd only spent one night outside, but Esther had been fending for herself for a long time. When they got home Selene would help her get the mats out of her coat, and Margaret would get her a flea collar so she wouldn't have to

scratch so much. *If* they got home. Then she looked up and saw the sea gull soaring overhead. Or perhap it was one of his cousins. "Hey!" she called, "could you help me? I need directions. . . ."

The sea gull flapped his wings and flew higher. Then Selene had an idea. Sea gulls lived near the water. That must be the right direction. She set out at a good clip, and Esther swung into step beside her. Together they walked almost all day in the direction the sea gull had flown. By late afternoon they came in sight of the bay.

Selene stopped and twitched her tail with satisfaction. "There," she said, pointing toward the houseboat marina. "That's where I live!" Selene's pads were sore from walking all day on concrete and asphalt, but she didn't have far to go now, so she and Esther loped along with renewed vigor.

At the door of her houseboat, Selene meowed loudly. The door swung open and Margaret scooped her up and stroked her with warm, comforting fingers. "Selene, I'm *so* glad to see you. I was worried sick about you. I was about to call the Missing Cat Bureau. Are you all right? Where have you been?"

Selene tried to explain it to Margaret and introduced her to Esther.

"What a pretty calico cat!" Margaret exclaimed. "How nice that you found a friend!" Then she gave each of them two dishes—one of milk and one of chopped liver.

"See?" Selene asked Esther. "I told you Margaret would be happy to see you."

Later, Margaret combed out Esther's coat and fastened a flea collar around her neck. It made Esther itch and jump. She ran all over the houseboat, trying to get

away from the discomfort.

Selene ran after her and licked her coat with her tongue. "Soon they'll go away. You'll feel much better then."

Esther sighed with relief. "I already do," she said.

Selene kept stroking her with her tongue and Esther purred with contentment. "Oh, look," she said to Selene.

Selene looked outside where Esther was looking. All she saw was the same old stuff—the houseboat next door, the ropes that tied them to the pilings, the boats and birds out in the bay.

"Those ropes," Esther said. "Wouldn't it be fun to play on them? We could swing back and forth, run up them to the dock, have a wonderful time."

"We could," Selene said. She'd seen those ropes every day since she'd lived there, but she'd never thought about how much fun they might be. "Let's do it tomorrow," she suggested, already picturing herself and Esther hanging upside down from the ropes, then swinging upright and scampering along up to the dock. On the dock they'd play tag, hide-and-go-seek, and who knew what else?

"I can't wait," Esther said with a big yawn, "but right now—"

Just then they heard a soft *plonk* on the deck outside. And then another. When Selene and Esther went to investigate they found two mussels, neatly shelled, sitting on the deck.

"The dinner Margaret gave us was quite delicious," Esther declared, "but so are these mussels. Did they come from the sky?"

"No. I believe they came from a—ah—a friend of mine," answered Selene. She looked up and saw a whir of white. Then she heard someone calling, "Welcome back."